Horseshoes
#1

The Perfect
HORSE

Horseshoes
#1

The Perfect
HORSE

Written by Patricia Leitch

HarperTrophy

A Division of HarperCollins*Publishers*

This series is for Meg

First published in Great Britain by Lions, an imprint of
HarperCollins Publishers, in 1992.

THE PERFECT HORSE
Copyright © 1992 by Patricia Leitch
For information address HarperCollins Children's Books,
a division of HarperCollins Publishers,
10 East 53rd Street, New York, NY 10022.

Library of Congress Cataloging-in-Publication Data
Leitch, Patricia
The perfect horse / written by Patricia Leitch
p.   cm. — (Horseshoes ; #1)
Summary: When she and her family move to a huge old manor
house in northern Scotland, ten-year-old Sally hopes to be able to
get the horse of her dreams.
ISBN 0-06-027289-9 (lib. bdg.) — ISBN 0-06-440634-2 (pbk.)
[1. Horses—Fiction.   2. Moving, Household—Fiction.
3. Scotland—Fiction.]   I. Title.   II. Series: Leitch, Patricia.
Horseshoes ; #1.
PZ7.L5372Pe   1996   95-26350
[Fic]—dc20   CIP
                                                                AC

Typography by Darcy Soper
2   3   4   5   6   7   8   9   10
❖
First Edition

Also by Patricia Leitch

HORSESHOES #2
JUMPING LESSONS

Chapter One

The Lorimer family all shared the same dream. They all dreamed that someday, when they had a lot of money, they would buy Kestrel Manor and live there. Kestrel Manor was a huge old house with battlements and a high stone tower. It was surrounded by overgrown gardens, and on one side there was a field that was just right for horses. It was built on a peninsula—almost an island—that jutted out into the sea, joined to the mainland only by a long, broad avenue lined with copper beech trees.

Mr. Lorimer, who was a librarian, imagined himself turning the wild grounds into a garden, growing fruits and vegetables and flowers. Mrs. Lorimer saw herself filling cupboards with jars of homemade jam, pickles, and canned fruit, or sitting at the top of the tower painting views of the sea and countryside.

Ben Lorimer was fifteen and tall for his age,

with a shock of black hair like his father's. He wanted a room to himself, a room lined with shelves for his books, a room where no one would disturb him.

Jamie Lorimer was four and the youngest Lorimer. He imagined life at Kestrel Manor being nothing but ice cream, sand castles, and swimming (with one foot securely on the sand, of course).

Meg Lorimer was a black-and-white Bearded collie. She was twelve years old and spent most of her waking hours staring at things and barking for attention. Misty Lorimer was a light-gray-and-white Beardie. She was five, with big brown eyes gleaming through her shaggy fur, and she loved to run. If you looked away for a second, Misty was off on some private exploration of her own.

But Sally Lorimer, who was ten—medium height: not small, not tall; medium size: not fat, not skinny; with thick brown bangs and hair that fell straight to her shoulders, wide-set blue eyes, and a quirky mouth that turned up at the corners—Sally longed to live at Kestrel Manor more than all the rest of her family put together. Because no one, absolutely no one, could live in a house that had stalls, outbuildings, and a field that only needed fencing to be the perfect horse field; no one could live at Kestrel Manor and not have a horse.

So her father wouldn't forget that Sally wanted a horse more than anything else in the world, Sally mentioned it to him quite often. But she hadn't really much hope. The Lorimers lived in Matwood, a suburb of Tarent in the northwest of Scotland. The squashed backyard of their town house was not really the place for a horse, nor were the busy local roads much good for riding. Even Miss Meek's riding school, where Sally rode when she had saved up enough pocket money, was only two bare fields wired off into grazing strips and a rutted lane that the school horses knew so well they could almost lead the rides themselves.

When Sally had first seen Kestrel Manor, she had known at once that this was the place for her horses—the imaginary horses that she rode everywhere. She saw Starfire, her chestnut stallion, standing in the field with proudly arched neck and alert ears, while Biddy, her trusty bay mare, dozed in the shadow of the chestnut tree. Sally trotted Lucia, her snow-white mare, up the long avenue under the purple shadows of the beeches, Meg and Misty leaping beside them.

But that was only make-believe.

The Lorimers had discovered Kestrel Manor a year before. They had been looking for a new picnic place when Mr. Lorimer stopped the car at the gates of Kestrel Manor. A cracked, weather-beaten sign said that the house was for sale, although the real-estate agent's name had almost vanished and the sign telling them that trespassers would be prosecuted was lying half hidden in the long grass.

"Shall we have a look?" Mrs. Lorimer asked, peering up the long avenue.

"Why not?" Mr. Lorimer said, and they all piled out of the car.

They walked for the first time under the beeches and up to the securely locked oak door at the foot of the tower. Four windows stretched above them to the top of the tower. To the right and left, ivy-covered walls reached up to the battlements. On either side of the door were two huge stone dogs, one sitting upright, the other lying down with its massive head stretched out on massive paws.

"Like dogs from a fairy tale," said Ben as Meg and Misty sniffed them suspiciously.

They walked around the house to the right of the tower and found themselves in a cobbled stable yard. On one side were four stalls and on the other side was a range of stable buildings.

"*The* place for your horse," Ben said to Sally.

But Sally was standing wide-eyed and unbelieving. To live at Kestrel Manor and have your own stable yard! For a moment she thought she saw shadowy heads gazing with gentle eyes over half doors, and thought she heard hooves trampling on straw. Then the air quivered and they were gone. Sally rubbed her eyes, not knowing whether she had seen horses that had been stabled there in the past or glimpsed the future horses that would come one day to stand in these empty stalls.

There was a walled garden festooned with roses and drenched in their scent, a ruined greenhouse of broken glass and twisted metal, and a vegetable garden that still had rhubarb and potatoes growing among the weeds. At the back of the house a field that must once have been a broad green lawn reached down to a desolate summerhouse that perched high above the sea.

For a long moment the Lorimers stood in the summerhouse surrounded by sea and sky in a glory of light and space, staring out into the silence.

Then Mrs. Lorimer turned to her husband and said, "We must buy it. We must come and live here. Oh, Rob, we must," almost as if she had been Sally pleading desperately for a horse.

But when Mr. Lorimer tracked down the real-estate agent who was selling Kestrel Manor, it was so terribly expensive that they all knew they could never afford to buy it.

"When we win the lottery," Mrs. Lorimer said, defeated.

Only Sally had not given up. Whenever the thought of Kestrel Manor came into her head, she saw herself riding her own horse up the avenue to where her whole family leaned over the battlements, waving down to her. She saw it all in color. Her horse was dapple-gray with a white mane and tail.

She was sure it would happen. They would live at Kestrel Manor . . . one day.

Chapter Two

The Lorimers had their first picnic of the year at Fintry Bay, a sandy beach close to Kestrel Manor. It was a day of blue sky, and the sun felt warm for the first time in months.

Mr. Lorimer pulled his tweed cap over his eyes and lay back on the sand. Mrs. Lorimer got out her watercolors and covered pages of her sketch pad with blues and greens. Ben sat on the seawall reading, pretending he didn't belong to his family. Jamie made sand castles, sat on a jellyfish, screamed, and then made more sand castles. The Beardies barked and leaped and barked. They plunged through the seaweed, found a very dead seagull and rolled in it, and had to be washed off in the sea.

All afternoon Sally sat with her arms wrapped around her knees, watching the path that came down to the sand. It was the way a nearby riding school came when they rode on the beach. Sally had seen them quite often. The girl who led the rides was very slim, with tanned skin and dark hair. She wore a black jacket and boots with buff breeches. Usually she rode a well-schooled black horse with one white sock and a broad white blaze, but once Sally had seen her on a chestnut that bucked and reared when he felt sand under his hooves. The girl had controlled him effortlessly, telling the other riders to trot on while she steadied the chestnut to a long, striding walk.

The riders were always neatly turned out, and their horses shone with grooming and good feeding. Not in the least like Miss Meek's dusty ponies.

But today there was no sign of the riding school. Only a girl on a bay cob had cantered past.

"Time we were making a move?" Mr. Lorimer asked, not moving himself.

"Well, if we're going to go by Kestrel Manor . . ." said Mrs. Lorimer.

But still nobody moved. The low sun was warm. The road back home would be busy.

"Four months since we've seen Kestrel Manor," Sally thought. "Anything could have happened. It could have been sold, or it might have been pulled down and little cottages built in its place."

Sally pictured Kestrel Manor gaunt and empty, unloved. She whispered the name Starfire, and her chestnut stallion came skimming over the beach. Sally leaped onto his back, and in seconds she was cantering up the avenue to Kestrel Manor.

"Hand me that basket," her mother said, shattering Sally's dream.

Sally handed the picnic basket to her mother and stood up.

"Where are you going?" her mother asked, as if Sally might have been setting off for Mars.

"Just down to the sea."

"Don't be long. We're going."

Sally scuffed her bare feet through the sand and paddled through the crimpling froth of the waves. Not to be living at Kestrel Manor seemed such a stupid waste. She didn't want to go back to their brick box home. She wanted to live by the sea for always. She wanted to catch her dapple-gray horse—not a pretend horse but a real horse—and ride bareback over the sand, her horse's silver mane and tail flowing as they galloped.

Suddenly the setting sun tipped the horizon and instantly a path of golden light stretched out from the sun to the foam's edge.

"Sally, come on," called her mother. "Hurry up."

Sally hardly heard her. She turned to face the sun. Standing in the sea, facing the golden light, she opened her arms wide.

"A horse," she said aloud. "I, Sally Lorimer, wish for a horse."

"Goofball," said Ben's voice behind her. "What would you do if a horse came trotting out of the waves? Keep it in the garage?"

Sally hunched her shoulders against her brother's stupidity. For of course she would keep it at Kestrel Manor.

Taking one last blinding look at the sun, Sally reluctantly turned to go. But as she turned away, something glittering under the water caught her eye. She crouched down to pick it up, and the movement of the sea carried it into the palm of her open hand, almost as if it had swum there by itself. Sally lifted her hand out of the water. Lying in the very center of her palm was a crystal unicorn.

It was about two inches high, with a gold horn and a gold tassel on its tail. Its tiny jewel eyes glinted red and green. It was not chipped or broken in any way.

"What have you found?" Ben demanded.

"Nothing," said Sally, closing her hand and spinning around. She raced across the beach to where her family was organizing the car.

"Some smell from those Beardies," said Mr. Lorimer when at last they were all packed in. The two dogs were mounded together between the backseat and the hatchback, in a wet sea-weedy mass of gray and black hair.

Sally stretched her arm over the backseat, trying to reach Meg and give her a comforting scratch.

"Don't get them excited," said her mother. "Let them settle down."

"Are we going past Kestrel Manor on the way home?" asked her father, knowing the answer before he asked.

"Yes. Yes. Yes," said Sally.

"I think we might," said Mrs. Lorimer.

Ben nodded his head, not looking up from his book. Only Jamie said nothing. He was asleep.

As they drove along the shore road to Kestrel Manor, they gradually stopped talking, each thinking the same thing but afraid to say it aloud. It was months since they had seen Kestrel Manor. Every hour of every day had been an hour when someone else might have bought their house.

But when Mr. Lorimer stopped at the rusted gates, the FOR SALE sign was still there.

"What will we do," said Sally, speaking for them all, "when we come and the sign is gone?"

"Go home and get our supper," said Ben. "I'm starving."

"Oh, no!" cried Sally. "Can't we just walk around once? Please?"

"No," said her mother. "Not tonight. It really is too late. Now that spring's here, we'll be able to come anytime. Anyway, we know that it's not sold, and that's the main thing."

Sally stared down the long, mossy avenue, fighting back tears. "Oh, please?" she pleaded, but her father was already looking over his shoulder to make sure the road was clear.

Suddenly Sally remembered the unicorn. She put her hand in her jacket pocket and felt it, tiny and magical. Instantly, instead of feeling sad at leaving Kestrel Manor without even walking up to the house, she was filled with fizzy, undeserved happiness.

"Look, Sally, a horse," said her mother.

Coming up the road was a girl of about Sally's age riding a finely bred roan horse. The girl was lean and tall. She sat easily astride her horse, riding with a relaxed confidence. Her black hard hat had aged to shades of green and was held on top of her sunburst of corn-colored hair by black elastic under her chin. Although her jeans and checked shirt looked worn, her tack was polished and her horse was fit and well groomed. Dazzles of white flickered over his sleek brownish-gray quarters. His hooves were oiled. His pulled mane and wisped tail fell in silken, separate hairs. Thinking of Miss Meek's riding-school ponies, Sally was filled with admiration.

Seeing that Mr. Lorimer was about to drive away, the girl halted. With an ear-to-ear grin, she waved Mr. Lorimer on. Sally, pushing Meg and Misty aside, rubbed the steamed-up rear window clear and watched the girl as they drove off.

"She's going to Kestrel Manor!" she exclaimed.

"She's probably just going for a ride around," said Mrs. Lorimer. "I expect there are lots of people who think of Kestrel Manor as their own."

But Sally wasn't listening. She was trotting Starfire beside the roan, riding as effortlessly and as confidently as the girl with the explosion of dark golden hair.

That night, before she went to bed, Sally placed the little unicorn on her windowsill. Rays of light from the street lamp caught it, making it shimmer with rainbows.

"Such a special thing," Sally thought, gazing at it. "Such a magical thing to come specially to me. Anything, anything, could happen now."

Chapter Three

The next magic thing happened on Friday morning. Mr. Lorimer and Ben had already left—Mr. Lorimer to his library and Ben to school. Mrs. Lorimer, who helped at Jamie's nursery school, was frantically trying to find red things for the red corner. Jamie was eating fistfuls of cornflakes from the box. Sally was searching madly for her spelling book.

"I have to find it. It must be somewhere. Miss MacGregor will climb the curtains if I don't have it," moaned Sally.

"Have you tried under your bed?" suggested her mother, just as there was a loud ring at the door.

"See who's there," Mrs. Lorimer said.

When Sally opened the door, it was the postman. He had two brown envelopes in his hand and one large white one.

"Is your dad here?" he asked, giving Sally the two brown envelopes. "He's got to sign for this one. Something special."

Mrs. Lorimer came to sign for the letter. Sally took it from the postman. It wasn't only the size that was special, everything about it was totally different from her father's usual letters. Mr. Lorimer's name and address had been typed by the kind of typewriter that made it look as if it were printed. On the back flap the name of the sender was pressed into the soft paper.

MARK & ROTH GOODCHILD

ATTORNEYS-AT-LAW

9 BREAM PLACE

TARENT G69 4X2

"Look at the time," screamed Mrs. Lorimer, snatching the envelope from Sally and standing it on the mantelpiece. "And I've got the keys to the nursery school! Hordes of little ones stranded on the sidewalk! Now, come on!"

"But I haven't got my spelling book. . . ."

"Then you'll need to share."

"But Miss MacGregor—"

"Out," said their mother, snatching Jamie up under her arm.

"*Out!*" she commanded, pushing Sally through the door and locking it behind her.

Mrs. Lorimer and Jamie turned left to their nursery school. Sally went straight on toward the concrete-and-glass school building. Now that her mother had left, Sally let Starfire gallop on the spot. His silver shoes struck sparks from the pavement, and his wild whinnyings soared above the brick houses, above the church steeple, and up to the golden disc of the sun. Mrs. Lorimer didn't like Sally imagining she was riding wild, uncontrollable horses. She wasn't even too crazy about Sally trotting along on a quiet pony.

Sally slid down from Starfire's back and stood still to watch her fiery stallion rear and plunge before he went soaring over the rooftops to Kestrel Manor and the sea.

School got out at four. Sally walked home alone, thinking about the letter. Meg and Misty, flopped at the back door, rose up to meet her with licks and paws. Sally sat down on the step and hugged them.

"Your school skirt," yelled her mother.

"Sorry. Forgot."

Meg and Misty followed Sally into the kitchen.

The envelope was still on the mantelpiece.

"Dad wasn't home at lunchtime?" Sally asked.

"This is his early night," said her mother.

Mr. Lorimer and Ben arrived home at twenty to five.

"There's a letter for you," said Sally as Mrs. Lorimer came running downstairs to tell her husband the same thing.

"Everyone calm down," said Mr. Lorimer, disentangling himself from Jamie's tackle embrace.

He took the letter and turned it over in his hands, reading the lawyers' names and address.

"Oh, open it, open it," said Mrs. Lorimer. "We've been waiting all day to find out what's in it."

"To do honor to this envelope I need a letter opener."

Sally brought a knife from the kitchen drawer.

"And my glasses."

"Where?" said Mrs. Lorimer.

"Briefcase."

Mrs. Lorimer found them and gave them to him.

Mr. Lorimer put them on and with a grand

gesture slit the envelope open with the kitchen knife. Very slowly he unfolded the sheet of thick white paper and read the letter aloud.

" 'Dear Sir, If you would contact me at the above address you will learn something to your advantage. As it is a matter of some urgency, I would be obliged if you would contact me as soon as possible. Graham Goodchild.' "

" 'To your advantage,' " said Ben. "That means it's good news."

"I don't believe it," said Mr. Lorimer. "Letters like this only happen in books."

The Beardies sensed the excitement and rioted around, barking at the top of their lungs.

"Get to the phone quick. It's only five to five. You might just catch them before they close." Mrs. Lorimer pushed her husband out into the hall to the phone.

Mr. Lorimer dialed the lawyer's number.

"Shut those dogs up. I can't hear. . . . Oh, yes, yes. Hello. Hello. It's Mr. Lorimer speaking," said Mr. Lorimer, signaling wildly to his wife to remove the Beardies.

Ben grabbed Meg and Mrs. Lorimer dragged Misty back into the kitchen.

Sally was still sitting on the edge of the table. To her the letter sounded like the beginning of some unicorn magic. Magic that might mean more riding lessons at Miss Meek's, or even a new jacket. She didn't dare to think that it might be strong enough magic to mean a horse.

"They've been trying to trace me for weeks," said Mr. Lorimer, coming back into the kitchen. "It was Mr. Goodchild himself who spoke to me. He wouldn't tell me anything at all over the phone, but he's opening the office tomorrow morning so he can see me at eleven o'clock."

"What can it be?" said Mrs. Lorimer.

"I have no idea," said Mr. Lorimer.

All night long Sally tossed and turned, trying to imagine what vitally important thing the lawyer was going to tell her father. She got up at six and took the dogs for a walk behind the school playground. Misty did her usual disappearing act, vanishing into thin air while Sally was tying her shoelace. For half an hour Sally searched and called, part of her furious that Misty had managed to get away and part of her desperately worried in case she should wander into the road and be run over.

At last Misty reappeared, wriggling her way through somebody's hedge. Her shaggy coat was tangled with mud and marigolds. She carried a crust of bread clamped firmly between her jaws.

"Where have you been?" raged Sally. "You wicked, wicked dog. Come here at once."

Misty advanced, one paw at a time, gulping down the bread.

Sally pounced and clipped on her leash.

"Does Meg ever go off on her own like that?" Sally demanded as she marched both dogs home. "No. It's always you dogging off. You are bad."

Misty smiled up at her, eyes wide, tail wagging uncertainly.

"Bad," repeated Sally, but a smile was creeping into her voice. Actually, Misty was her favorite.

Mr. Lorimer left for Tarent at half past nine. When Sally had tidied her bedroom, she went over to the riding school to fill the time until her father got back.

A ride was just ready to leave the yard.

Miss Meek was sitting solid and secure on a bay hunter called Fred.

"How would you like to clean up the stalls?" she called down to Sally.

Sally nodded, but stood watching the riders leave the yard. The boy on Tansy had one stirrup shorter than the other. Jane Ford, who was riding Clover, Sally's favorite pony, had her heels clamped against Clover's sides and her reins gathered up in a stranglehold that pulled the bit back against Clover's mouth. Prince and Princess were already lagging behind, ignoring their riders' crops and heels. They knew that if they stayed far enough behind the rest, they wouldn't have to go to the end of the lane.

As Sally turned away to find a brush, she saw the golden-haired girl's roan clearly in her mind. He was full of life and energy, trotting under the beeches to Kestrel Manor.

Sally had just finished three stalls when the riders came back. She helped the boy on Tansy to dismount and held Mint's leading rein until Miss Meek took it from her. Her watch said twelve o'clock. There was a chance that her father might be home.

At first Sally started to gallop home on Starfire, but somehow today she couldn't be bothered. Abandoning her stallion, she ran full tilt for home, her hand in her jacket pocket clenched around the unicorn.

Sally had almost reached their house when her father drew up at the gate. Instead of getting out, he just sat behind the wheel. The expression on his face was a blank mask of bewilderment. Even when he saw Sally, he didn't smile or wave. He just sat staring through the windshield. "Dad! Hi, Dad," Sally shouted. She had never seen her father like this before and she didn't know what to do. She couldn't go into the house and leave him sitting in the car.

"Dad?" she said again, uncertainly, but still Mr. Lorimer paid no attention to her. It was only when the Beardies came bounding and barking down the path that Mr. Lorimer got out of the car.

"Be quiet," he yelled at the dogs. "Stop that noise."

"What did the lawyer say? What's to your advantage?" Sally demanded.

Mr. Lorimer shut the gate, keeping Meg and

Misty in. He caught Sally around the waist and threw her into the air as if she were Jamie.

"Come on in," he said, catching her. "Then I'll tell you."

And as they ran up the path together, he laughed and laughed as if he would never stop.

Chapter Four

Mrs. Lorimer was standing at the sink, peeling potatoes. Jamie was sitting on the floor with one potato and a blunt knife, helping her.

"Well?" she demanded.

"Are you sitting comfortably?" asked her husband.

"Don't be silly! Tell me!"

Ben, hearing his father's voice, came racing down from his room.

Mr. Lorimer drew in a deep breath.

"I've been left a considerable sum of money," he said.

"You've what?" said his wife.

"The lawyer's own words. 'A considerable sum of money.' In fact you might say quite a lot of money."

"Go on," said Mrs. Lorimer. "You're joking."

"How much?" said Ben.

"A considerable sum," repeated Mr. Lorimer, and Sally saw a quick glance pass between her parents. Clearly the details of the considerable amount were not going to be family information.

Mrs. Lorimer sat down hard on a chair.

"I don't believe it. It couldn't happen to us."

"It's happened. Dad's great-uncle Nathan died last December. I hardly knew him. He went off to Australia when he was sixteen. Came back to see us twice. He had red hair and took me to a soccer match and that's all I remember about him. He used to send us a Christmas card and a letter to Dad now and again. He'd bought a sheep farm. Seemed to have done well. Never married. Since Dad died I've never heard from him, and now—pow!— out of the blue. I am his only living relative, so everything comes to me."

In the blank silence that followed Mr. Lorimer's words, Sally searched in her pocket, found the crystal unicorn, and squeezed it tightly in her hand. She was almost afraid of it. It had worked so much magic in a week! If they really had inherited a lot of money, it made a horse of her own not only possible but almost certain.

"Do you think perhaps . . ." she began at exactly the same moment that Ben started to say something about bookcases. But it was Mrs. Lorimer who got the words out first.

"Kestrel Manor?" she said.

"Why not?" said Mr. Lorimer. He put his hand in his pocket and brought out three keys on a ring attached to a label. "Thought one of you might suggest it, so I popped into the real-estate agent's and got the keys."

Suddenly everyone was talking and laughing, all at the same time, while the Beardies leaped about in crazy, Chinese-dragon cascades of hair.

"Can we go there now?" Sally asked.

"I'll make up a picnic," said Mrs. Lorimer, bouncing Jamie on her knee and telling him that they were going to live in a castle.

"Will there be dungeons?" he asked. "Dragons?"

"Well, cellars," said his mother. "And most definitely frogs."

"Not the day for ordinary sandwiches," said Mr. Lorimer. "We'll stop at the supermarket and you can each fill a basket with whatever you like."

When they had all filled their baskets, Mr. Lorimer picked a bottle of champagne from the shelf.

"No glasses," said Ben, so they went to the aisle that had paper cups.

"We've come into a fortune," Sally told the assistant, because she had to tell someone.

"And pigs might fly," said the girl, not even smiling. Suddenly Sally saw pigs of all colors of the rainbow flying lumpily about the sky. Pigs that changed into horses, horses that galloped and reared and flung their heels into the air as if the whole sky were a daisy meadow.

"We can drive right up to the house now that it's ours," said Sally when they reached Kestrel Manor. "Our house."

"Don't count your chickens," said Mrs. Lorimer. "It may be in such a terrible condition that we won't be able to consider buying it."

"That's not what the man at the real-estate agent's said. He's coming down in the afternoon to show us around."

Meg and Misty had their heads out the car window. Sally pushed them out of the way to get a better view. The gray tower of Kestrel Manor, with its paved forecourt and guardian stone dogs, was waiting for them. She glanced back along the avenue and saw it was pitted with hoofprints.

Had the girl on the roan made them? Sally wondered. Perhaps she rode there a lot. And Sally realized that when—not *if,* but *when*—they came to live at Kestrel Manor, she was bound to get to know the girl and her roan. She'd know their names. She'd even ride with them when she had her own horse!

They all stood grouped around Mr. Lorimer as he unlocked the door. It groaned open and they found themselves looking into a huge hallway. A wide wooden staircase flowed down toward them. Each of its newel posts was topped with a little kestrel hawk carved in wood.

"Kestrel Manor," said Mr. Lorimer as they walked through the doorway for the first time. Sally's family paused at the foot of the staircase admiring the carvings, but Sally ran on, stirring the carpet of dust from the wooden stairs. At the very top of the stairs, hanging from an almost invisible wire, was a hovering kestrel, its wings outspread.

"Bet he loved them," said Mr. Lorimer,

catching up with Sally. "The man who carved them. They're almost alive."

"Is that the trapdoor to the tower?" Ben asked, pointing upward.

"Could be," agreed Mr. Lorimer. He lifted Sally onto his shoulders.

She could reach the trapdoor just enough to push it open. When the clouds of dust had settled, she could see a staircase spiraling upward to a platform at the top of the tower. Some of the steps had fallen away; others clung on in rotting tatters of wood.

"No use," said Sally. "You could never climb up it. But it is the tower. I can see the sky."

"Looks terribly dangerous to me," said Mrs. Lorimer, peering upward. "From this moment on it is totally forbidden."

Sally let down the trapdoor with a bang, and the dust clouds nearly choked them.

"Quick," said Ben. "To the summerhouse before we all suffocate—or starve."

Seen from the summerhouse, the sea flickered in dancing diamonds of light. Each of the Lorimers found a place on the decaying window seats and began to unpack the picnic.

"First," said Mr. Lorimer, "a toast."

They stood up, holding out their paper cups to be filled with champagne.

"To Great-uncle Nathan, wherever he is. May he know the joy he is giving us."

"Great-uncle Nathan," they chorused.

As Sally lifted the cup to her lips, tasting the not-sweet taste and bubbles of the champagne, she got goose bumps. Shivering, she suddenly knew that this was all for real. They really were coming to live here. She would need to change schools. She might never ride at Miss Meek's again. They were all going to leave the house where Sally had always lived. The horse she had dreamed about for so long was going to change from a make-believe horse into a real live horse. And she would be responsible for it. There would be no Miss Meek keeping an eye on things.

Suddenly Sally wasn't hungry. Even her bag of goodies didn't tempt her. She ate some smoked salmon to stop her mother from nagging her, and then she stood up.

"I'm going for a walk," she said, hoping

desperately that no one would offer to come with her. No one did. They were all too busy eating and talking. Even Meg and Misty did no more than roll their eyes at her, hardly daring to look away from the food.

Sally walked toward Kestrel Manor, finding her way to the stables. After their first discovery of the stables, the Lorimers had kept away from the house and outbuildings, somehow feeling that they would be trespassing more if they prowled around the house than if they just wandered around the grounds.

Sally stopped at the entrance to the stable yard. She stared around at the stalls and the buildings that must once have been feed houses and tack rooms. As if in a dream, she walked forward and looked into the first empty stall and then the next. The stone floors were covered with dirt and dust, and the walls festooned with dense cobwebs.

Sally crossed to the other side of the yard. She looked in through a door that was half open. There, alarming because they were so totally unexpected, were four bales of hay and an open bin half full of oats. On the wall hung polished tack. It was all exactly as Sally imagined it would be when she had her own horse to keep there. Sally clenched her eyes shut. When she opened them again, nothing had changed. She swung around, ready to dash back to the summerhouse and tell her parents what she had found, when a trumpeting whinny ripped the air. There was a sound of hooves on stone, and suddenly a roan's head with pricked ears and glistening eyes appeared over one of the stall doors. The horse crashed his front hooves against the door and whinnied again.

"Tarquin! Behave yourself!" Coming into the yard, carrying a bucket of water, was the girl with the sunburst of golden hair—the roan's rider.

Chapter Five

The two girls stared at each other in amazement. Sally couldn't imagine what the girl was doing stabling her horse at Kestrel Manor, but it didn't seem right. She was about to say hello when the girl spoke.

"You're trespassing," she said. "This is private property. You shouldn't be here."

Although the girl's voice sounded bossy, Sally thought her eyes looked guilty.

"You'd better go home," the girl was saying when they both heard a man's footsteps coming toward the yard. "Who's that?" she asked. "Someone with you?"

Sally shook her head. She knew it wasn't her father. In an instant the girl had dashed across the yard and slammed the door shut on the hay and oats. She was just in time. A second later a middle-aged man wearing a suit and city shoes walked into the yard.

"Afternoon," he said. "I heard your voices. You must be the Lorimer girls."

Sally nodded.

"I'm Mr. Scott, from the real-estate agent's," he said as he came across the yard toward them. Suddenly Tarquin neighed his impatience and clattered his hooves against the door.

"Good heavens!" said Mr. Scott, turning pink with shock. "Is that a horse? Don't tell me you've brought a horse with you!"

Mr. Scott marched past the girls and stared into the stall. "Well, you seem to have made yourself at home," he said. "Moved in already, have you?"

The roan was standing on a thin bed of straw. Straw from last night's bed was piled at the sides of the stall. An almost-empty hay net hung by the side of the manger.

"Your father doesn't own the place yet, you know. Actually, you have absolutely no right to do this sort of thing."

The girl with golden hair was staring down at her shoes, twisting her hands.

"We rode over," said Sally quickly.

"Well, make sure and clean up before you ride back. Now, where's your father?"

"They're in the summerhouse," said Sally.

With a last irritated glare at the horse, Mr. Scott hurried out of the yard.

"Gosh," said the girl. "That was close. Thanks for covering for me. I couldn't think of what to say. In another minute I'd have been telling him everything."

"What *is* everything?"

"Wait till I put the bucket in with Tarquin, and then I'll explain."

The roan ruffled his muzzle through the water but didn't drink.

"Typical," said the girl.

"He's a wonderful horse," said Sally, gazing in admiration, for Tarquin was as finely bred as a racehorse. His arched neck held aloft a fine-boned silken-skinned head with lustrous eyes, neat ears curved like shells, and a delicate muzzle. His mane was pulled to a light fringe and his tail fell in a neat tassel to just below his straight hocks. His smooth, iron-boned legs ended in small black hooves. He was completely different from any of Miss Meek's ponies. Totally and completely different from anything Sally had ever ridden.

"He is beautiful. You are lucky," Sally said,

and was about to explain how much she wanted her own horse but that there wasn't much hope, when she suddenly remembered that wasn't true any longer.

"I'm Thalia Nesbit. 'Thalia-rhymes-with-dahlia-which-is-a-flower-like-a-chrysanthemum.'"

"Oh," said Sally. "Well, I'm Sally Lorimer. My whole family's here. We're going to buy Kestrel Manor."

"What's your dad like? Will he let me go on keeping Tarquin here, or is he going to use all the stables for his racehorses? I couldn't possibly have left Tarquin outside all winter. He'd have frozen to death. I've only ever used this one stall. The hay and everything else is all mine. I delivered papers and walked dogs and I don't care what anyone says, I haven't done any harm."

"Didn't anybody know?"

"Only my grandmother. I live with her. In a cottage by the shore. No one else knows. They all thought I kept Tarquin in a field behind Narg's house. That's Gran spelled backward. When my mom had me, Narg said she wasn't going to be a grandmother but she would be a narg, that would suit her better."

As she spoke, Thalia's hazel eyes shone with excitement. She pushed her bony hands through her hair and chattered on as if she had known Sally all her life.

"But I'll be putting him out in the field during the day now that the weather is getting better. He's a present from Mom and Dad. When they split up, they gave me Tarquin. Of course, I'd always wanted a horse and I'd always spent a lot of time at Narg's, but all the same it was a bit weird—shattering my life and then giving me a horse."

"He looks really fast," said Sally.

"Oh, he is. Do you want a ride? I'm just going out."

"You wouldn't mind? Really? I'll need to tell Mom, but I'll run."

"Perhaps you could say something to your dad? About me?"

"He won't mind a bit," Sally assured her as she turned and ran out of the stable yard, taking great leaps over the long grass. A French window was standing open. As Sally raced up the three cracked, uneven steps, she could hear voices coming from the corridor beyond the drawing room.

Her family and Mr. Scott were standing in the huge kitchen.

Sally pulled at her mother's arm.

"I've met a friend," she said. "She's the girl on the roan. Can I go for a ride with her?"

"Don't you want to see the house? We couldn't find you."

"Mom, it's a horse."

"Well, be careful," said her mother. "Be sure to borrow her hard hat."

When Sally got back to the yard, Thalia had tacked up Tarquin and was standing outside waiting for her.

"Okay?"

"I've got to borrow your hat."

"It's soft as a pancake, but you can have a turn with it if you want. Did you ask?"

"I didn't have a chance. But he won't mind. Honest."

"Hope not," said Thalia. "Do you want to ride first? We can go down the track to the shore and ride on the beach."

Now that Tarquin was standing in the yard, he looked twice the height he had in his stall. Thalia was holding him by the length of his reins as he pranced sideways, clinking his bit impatiently and kicking up his heels.

Sally regarded him nervously. "If Thalia let go of his reins, he would gallop out of sight," she thought. She had only seen horses behaving like this on television. Even at their local show the horses usually plodded along quite calmly. But Tarquin wasn't like them. He was fire and lightning, and she was going to have to ride him.

"Perhaps you'd better go first," Sally said. "I don't know the way down to the beach."

"Right," said Thalia, taking Tarquin's reins over his head, checking his girth and pulling down his stirrups. "He is pretty fresh."

Effortlessly her long legs swung her into the saddle. "This way," she said, riding out of the yard.

The door where Thalia kept her feed was now securely locked. If Sally's parents and the real-estate agent came into the stable yard, they would see only the bed in Tarquin's stall. They would think it was being used only today.

Tarquin trotted down the narrow path to the shore.

"Tide's going out," said Thalia. "I usually school for a bit first. Then it'll be your turn, okay?"

Ignoring Tarquin's switching tail and shaking head, Thalia rode him firmly away from Sally and began to walk him in a wide circle. Gradually the horse began to pay attention to his rider, walking out with a long, reaching stride. Thalia squeezed her legs against his sides, and he changed smoothly into a slow sitting trot.

Watching, Sally knew that Thalia could really ride. In a few minutes she had changed a restive, unwilling horse into a calm, obedient one.

"I'll never be able to ride as well as that," Sally thought as she stared entranced at Tarquin and his rider silhouetted against the brightness of the sea. "Never."

"Right," said Thalia, walking Tarquin back to Sally. "Your turn."

Sally put on Thalia's hat. It sank down over her ears like a tea cozy.

"Have you ridden a lot?" Thalia asked as Sally climbed into the saddle. In her excitement Sally had forgotten to put the toe of her shoe against the girth and had poked Tarquin in the ribs, making him leap sideways.

"At Miss Meek's riding school," said Sally, shortening her stirrups. She thought fondly of the riding school ponies, who always stood like blocks of wood while riding crops flapped about their faces and new jodhpur boots gouged into their sides.

"Take him along the beach," said Thalia, letting go of Tarquin's bridle. "Give him a canter."

Sally gathered up her reins as she always did on Miss Meek's ponies. Tarquin threw up his head and broke into a ragged trot.

"Careful with his mouth," Thalia shouted. "Don't hang on to him like that."

But her warning was too late. Feeling the unbalanced rider on his back, Tarquin trotted faster and faster.

"Steady, steady," Sally said. "Whoa, now."

Tarquin seemed so narrow between her knees. His neck reached upward, pointing his head at the sky so that Sally could see the whites of his eyes. She tried to switch her reins into one hand so that she could clap his neck, but they were a bulky jumble of leather that she couldn't sort out.

By now Tarquin was trotting faster than ever, far faster than a canter, the sand spurting from his hooves as if he were racing.

"Steady! Whoa!" pleaded Sally. "Stop! Oh, please stop!"

Helplessly she bumped up and down on his hard, fit back, not even able to post, hardly able to stay in the saddle.

In front of them was a rotted jetty. Tarquin pricked his sharp ears and thundered toward it.

"No!" screamed Sally, not caring who heard her. "Stop, Tarquin. Stop!" But Tarquin thundered on.

He leaped straight up into the air, straight over, and straight down again. Sally flew up out of the saddle and thumped down on his neck when they landed on the other side. As she struggled back into the saddle, Tarquin swung around on his hocks, battered around the end of the jetty, and then, as if a rocket had blasted him from behind, charged into a full gallop, his head low, his legs going like pistons.

Sally, clutching the reins and the pommel of

the saddle, clung on helplessly. The tiny figure of Thalia seemed miles away. As Tarquin raced toward his owner, Sally saw her family coming across the sand to join Thalia.

"Don't fall off, don't fall off," Sally told herself. "They'll never buy you a horse if they see you fall off."

Sally was completely out of control. There was nothing she could do to slow Tarquin down. If he wanted to gallop all the way back to the stables, Sally couldn't stop him. She could only cling, tight with terror.

But when they reached Thalia, Tarquin's gallop slowed to a canter. He stopped with three unseating bounces, making Sally clutch at handfuls of mane to stay on top. Sally waited, expecting everyone to start asking her what had gone wrong, but to her amazement no one was paying much attention to her. Thalia and her father were talking about stabling Tarquin. Mrs. Lorimer was holding Meg and Misty, trying to stop them from digging in the sand, while Ben and Jamie were grubbing about looking for shells and things.

"And you can keep him in the field in the

summer," Mr. Lorimer was saying to Thalia. "We'll be fencing it in for Sally's horse."

Sally slid down from Tarquin's back. She stood leaning against the horse, clutching his saddle to stop herself from collapsing onto the sand.

She had longed to hear her father say the words "Sally's horse" for many years. Sally's horse. Her own horse. But now she could do nothing but try to control her shaking arms, try to stop her legs from trembling, and wipe the tears off her face before anyone noticed.

"I'll come by and see your gran—sorry— narg. Fix things up," said Mr. Lorimer.

Thalia's thanks bubbled out of her.

"When the firing squad has you lined up, send for me and I'll take your place," she promised. Turning to Sally, she said, "He loves a gallop, doesn't he? You can have another if you like."

Sally swallowed hard. Her mother spoke for her.

"Another time," she said to Thalia. "We didn't know we were coming here until this morning. It's the Parents' Association supper tonight, so we've got to get back. But you'll have lots of time to get to know each other now that we're going to be your new neighbors."

On the way home to their house that wasn't home any longer, Sally sat in the back of the car, clutching an unwilling Misty on her knee. Squashed in by Ben, she listened to her family talking about all the things that they would do when they came to live at Kestrel Manor. But she couldn't join in.

Sally was still filled with the panic that had seized her when Tarquin had run away with her. She could so easily have been thrown over his head to crash facedown into the rotting wood and rusty iron of the jetty. She could so easily have come off and been dragged along behind him, her foot jammed in a stirrup, his hooves thundering about her head. Sally clutched Misty tighter and buried her face in the dog's comforting warmth.

But it wasn't until she was lying in bed that night that she faced up to the truth.

"Sally Lorimer," she said to herself. "You didn't want to ride Tarquin again, did you? You were glad you had to go home, weren't you?

"I'd never ridden a big, spirited, athletic horse like that before," Sally thought, making excuses for herself. "Never jumped like that before."

"You were afraid," said the voice in Sally's head, the voice that always spoke the truth. "Sally Lorimer, you are nothing but a coward."

Chapter Six

The next two weeks were the most frantic, exciting time that Sally had ever known. Everything about her old life was vanishing. Soon there would be nothing left of it. Things that had lain in cupboards utterly undisturbed for years were crammed into black plastic bags and thrown out. Plates and ornaments, pictures and books, all had to be wrapped and packed into boxes to wait for the movers.

Mr. Lorimer had sold their house to a fellow librarian who had just come up to Scotland from the south of England. He wanted to move in before his wife and family joined him. This meant the Lorimers had to move into Kestrel Manor as soon as possible.

Mrs. Lorimer and several of her friends scrubbed and swept and vacuumed Kestrel Manor while workmen carried out the most urgent repairs. Curtains and carpets were bought and fitted. Thalia's narg, who was short and stout and charged around on a motorbike,

set up a canteen in Kestrel Manor's kitchen.
She supplied everyone with soup, sandwiches,
and as much tea or coffee as they could drink.

"Most dear unknown Great-uncle Nathan,"
said Mr. Lorimer. "We could never have
afforded any of this without you. Thank you,
thank you, thank you."

One evening, with the move only four days
away, there was nothing really urgent that had
to be done.

"I shall put my feet up and watch television," said Mrs. Lorimer. "I even miss the com-
mercials."

"Since it's a nice evening, I thought Sally
and I might take a walk over to the riding
school," suggested Mr. Lorimer.

Sally looked up from her spelling list. She
hadn't been thinking about going to the riding
school tonight. She had been planning to buy
apples and carrots and say good-bye to the ponies
on Friday afternoon, after her last day at school.

"I gave Miss Meek a call at lunchtime, so
she'll be there tonight," said her father.

"Miss Meek is always there," said Sally.

"I mentioned to her that we were looking

for a horse for you. She agreed that it would be a good idea to look at one of hers."

Sally grinned with utter surprise, her eyes opened wide with delight.

"You mean it?" she gasped. "You really mean it?"

"I tell you no lies. She suggested Clover as a possible. Said she was your favorite."

Sally skipped along beside her father as they set off for the riding school.

"Pinch me," she kept saying. "Pinch me so I know it's real."

She could not believe that her dream was coming true. So many times she had ridden up and down the lane on Clover imagining that the pony belonged to her, and now . . .

Clover was standing tacked up in a stall. No one had bothered to give her a proper grooming. Her black coat was dull, and her white socks were their usual shade of yellowish green. Even her long tail and straggling mane had not been brushed out.

When Miss Meek opened the stall door, Clover looked at them with weary, lackluster eyes. She shifted her weight but made no attempt to walk toward them. Sally scratched her neck, spoke to her, and gave her a sugar lump. Miss Meek freed the reins from Clover's stirrup and led her into the yard.

"Up you go," she said to Sally. "Ride her down the lane."

While Sally mounted, Clover stood like a wooden horse—head down and resting a hind leg.

"Wake her up," warned Miss Meek. "She's not used to being taken out alone."

Sally turned the unwilling pony toward the lane and tried to kick her on. But Clover, with a sudden burst of energy, swung around and would have carried Sally back into the stall if Miss Meek hadn't caught her bridle.

"No!" she said to the pony, and led her to the beginning of the lane. There she clapped Clover hard on the rump and sent her off at a ragged trot.

"Keep her going," Miss Meek shouted at Sally. "Don't let her get the better of you like that. Kick her on."

Obediently Sally kicked her heels into Clover's wooden sides.

"It's only Clover you're on," she told herself severely, "not Tarquin." For when Clover had tried to carry her back into the stall, Sally had felt her heart tighten with the same panic she had felt when Tarquin ran away with her.

Sally rode at Clover's slow walk to the end of the lane.

"What's wrong with you, Sally Lorimer?" she asked herself. "Here you are riding your favorite pony and you're cross and cranky and . . ." Sally couldn't bring herself to add "scared," for what was there to be scared about when she was riding Clover? Scared that Clover would get out of control? Scared that Clover would run away with her?

When they reached the end of the lane, Clover turned, walked a few strides, trotted, and, at exactly the place where the riders always cantered, broke into an uneven rocking-horse canter. She trotted again at exactly the place where the riders always slowed to a trot. Back at the beginning of the lane Clover suggested that they should return to the yard. But Sally kicked and pulled at the reins, and after a moment's struggle Clover gave in and plodded back down the lane.

After she had ridden up and down the lane a few times, Sally rode back to the yard. When Clover was with the other riding-school ponies, Sally had enjoyed riding her, but riding her alone wasn't the same at all. Clover would always expect to be hit and kicked, expect heavy hands to tug on her reins, jabbing her in the mouth. That was the way she was always ridden. If she took Clover away from her lane, Sally didn't think she would be able to control her at all.

In the yard Miss Meek was telling her father that Clover would make an ideal pony for his daughter. Owning a pony was not the same as riding at a riding school, she said. And Clover, being perfectly reliable, would take good care of Sally.

"Well, how did she go for you?" asked Miss Meek, being briskly enthusiastic.

"Okay," said Sally. "Shall I take her tack off?"

"Put her in aisle five," Miss Meek told Sally when she brought Clover out of the stall.

Sally pulled the halter over Clover's ears and set her free. The pony waited to snatch Sally's offering of sugar lumps, then swung away to tear at the short, overgrazed grass.

Sally blinked hard. For a miserable second she saw Clover grazing in the newly fenced field at Kestrel Manor. She knew that she had only to say yes, she would love to have Clover, and that was what would happen. But she shook her head to clear the thought from her mind.

"Well, then?" said Mr. Lorimer in the tone of voice that showed that he thought everything was settled.

"No," said Sally, her throat so tight that she could hardly speak. "I don't want Clover. I'm sorry, but I really don't want a riding-school pony."

Sally scuffed her feet along the pavement. She couldn't find words to tell him that, much as she liked Clover, she didn't want a pony that was used to everyone riding it—a pony used to kicks and jabs in the mouth. The pony she was looking for had to be special.

"Don't upset yourself," said her father. "Lots of time to look around."

Sally smiled up at him gratefully. She would find her horse the way she had found her unicorn.

Chapter Seven

*T*hey moved to Kestrel Manor on a day of pouring rain. The movers were bad-tempered and the Beardies left wet, hairy footprints on the new carpets. Narg's soup kitchen was crowded out. Jamie sat under the table and ate a whole box of chocolate cookies.

The night before, Mrs. Lorimer had said that they must make up their minds about bedrooms.

"Dad and I have picked ours in the corridor to the right and there's a smallish room next to us for Jamie. Now, how about the rest of you?"

With one voice Ben and Sally said, "The room at the top of the stairs."

"I'm the eldest," stated Ben, seeing himself sitting in the room at the top of the stairs, surrounded by books.

"I'm the *girl*," said Sally.

"Fetch the straws," said Mr. Lorimer.

Ben brought two drinking straws. Mr. Lorimer cut the end of one of them, then held them out so that the straws looked even. You could not tell which was the short one.

"Short straw," said Mr. Lorimer. "Top room. Who wants to draw?"

"Oh, I want it so badly," Sally said.

"Get on with it, then," said Ben. "Stop messing around. I'm bound to win."

Sally gave the two straws a hard stare. One of them meant having the highest room in Kestrel Manor for her own. She imagined herself sitting in the window seat, staring out over the wild winter sea or, in the summer, being able to see right along the shoreline. Only from the top of the tower would there be a better view.

"Please, please," she whispered. Picturing her unicorn in her mind's eye, she screwed her eyes shut and grabbed one of the straws from her father's hand.

"Oh, no!" exclaimed Ben. "It's not fair."

And Sally knew that the top bedroom was hers.

On their first night at Kestrel Manor, Sally, sitting up in bed with Misty asleep at her feet, could see out across the water. She called to

Starfire and he came cantering over the water, then faded from Sally's sight like the dream he was. Biddy and Lucia, trotting behind him, vanished too. Things were real, now that the Lorimers' wish had come true.

That evening Sally had helped Thalia bed down Tarquin. Soon her own horse would be standing in the stall next to him. Not a riding-school pony nor an almost-Thoroughbred like Tarquin, but her own horse. With an electric shock of amazement Sally realized that her own horse must be somewhere, at this very moment, waiting for her to find it.

Sally closed her eyes, almost asleep, trying to imagine the horse that would be hers. At first she couldn't picture anything. Then Tarquin was there and at once she was riding him. The sounds of his pounding hooves mingled with her own screams as he bolted over the shore. And again Sally felt the terrible panic of being totally helpless.

She started awake and lay trembling, afraid to go to sleep again in case the nightmare was waiting for her.

Ben and Mr. Lorimer had to leave half an

hour earlier in the morning to get to school and work, and Sally was going to a new school. It was a small three-teacher school. Knowing Thalia made it all quite easy. She seemed to be popular with all the children and introduced Sally as her new friend.

"Well, you are," said Thalia when Sally tried to thank her. "But you'd be a better friend if you'd only hurry up and get a horse. I keep offering you rides on Tarquin, but you won't."

"When I have my own horse, we can ride together."

"But *when*? If only you'd keep working on your dad."

Sally did keep working on her father. Taking Thalia with them, they went to see a horse that was advertised in the local paper as a super safety ride. It turned out to be far too small for Sally.

"I think," said Mr. Lorimer as they drove away, "we need someone who knows about buying horses. I shall ask Miss Wevell. She often arrives at the library in her breeches, so I feel she must know about horses."

Miss Wevell was delighted to help. She knew

a Mr. Josh Frazer who had stables close to Kestrel Manor. She said she would phone him to see if he had any suitable horses for sale. If he did, she would come with them to give the horses the once-over.

When Thalia heard that they were going to Mr. Frazer's stables, she said at once that she was coming with them.

"It is *the* place," she said. "No one but the best goes there."

As they drove into Mr. Frazer's yard the next Saturday, Sally's heart sank. Thalia was right. It was the finest—a range of neatly painted stalls surrounded by an immaculate stable yard. There was not a wisp of straw or hay to be seen anywhere. Miss Wevell, Thalia, Sally, and Mr. Lorimer got out of the car. As if from thin air Mr. Frazer appeared, striding across the yard to greet them.

"Now then," he said when the introductions were over. "You're looking for a horse. Who is it for?"

"Sally, my daughter," said Mr. Lorimer.

"Ah, yes," said Mr. Frazer. He had a long, weather-beaten face with flat cheeks and bright blue eyes. "So you want your own horse? How much riding have you done?"

"Only at a riding school," said Sally, suddenly feeling very small.

"A beginner?" asked Mr. Frazer, turning to Mr. Lorimer.

"I think we might say that," agreed her father, smiling at Sally.

"Then I think I might have the very horse. Martine, bring out Bilbo, please."

A dark-haired girl wearing a black jacket, jodhpurs, and black boots went into one of the stalls. Sally was sure she had seen her somewhere before, but it wasn't until she was leading a stocky bay horse toward them that Sally remembered where. She was the girl who had been in charge of the rides that Sally had seen when they picnicked at Fintry Bay. The horses must have come from these stables.

Bilbo had a clipped mane, a white star, and a pink muzzle that pushed at Sally's pockets hoping for tidbits.

Sally patted his neck and told him that she hadn't anything for him, not liking to give him sugar lumps in front of Mr. Frazer.

"Right. What do you think of him?" said Mr. Frazer while Miss Wevell looked critically at the horse, running her hand down his sturdy legs and looking at his teeth in a knowledgeable way.

"Eight years old," said Mr. Frazer. "Totally genuine child's horse. Bring any vet you like to look at him. He's perfectly sound. The boy who had him outgrew him. His family bought his new horse from me and asked me to sell Bilbo for them."

Thalia whispered to Sally that he didn't look very fast to her and could he jump? Mr. Frazer asked Sally if she wanted to try him.

"Do you like him?" asked her father, and Sally nodded, her heart thumping in her throat with excitement.

"Up you go then," said Mr. Frazer. Feeling that they were all watching her, Sally was suddenly nervous. She almost wished that it was Thalia who had to ride Bilbo.

Sally mounted, and Mr. Frazer led the way to a grass paddock. Bilbo walked around with a steady, workmanlike stride. When Sally asked him to trot, he changed at once into a bouncy trot. When she had ridden him around in both directions, Sally asked him to canter and he changed without any fuss, hardly increasing his speed. He did not feel like a runaway type of horse at all.

"There you are," said Mr. Frazer. "Goes well for you. No need to be nervous." Sally wondered how he knew.

"Need to try him on the road in traffic," said Miss Wevell, who knew all about horses.

"There's a ride going out in a quarter of an hour," said Mr. Frazer. "Sally can join them. Martine Dawes is leading the ride, so she'll be in safe hands."

Sally rode at the front of the ride beside Martine Dawes, who was riding her black horse. Behind them were two teenage boys, four women, and a girl a bit older than Sally on a piebald horse.

The horses' hooves made a grand clatter on the flat shore road. Even when they trotted, Bilbo kept up easily with Martine's black horse. He looked about him with a bright, self-assured intelligence, and when Sally spoke to him his black-tipped ears flickered back and forward at the sound of her voice.

"He's going well for you," said Martine. "Nice horse. He'd suit you."

Sally sat up straighter than ever, trying hard to remember all Miss Meek's instructions. She was just settling into enjoying herself when Martine stood up in her stirrups and looked back at the other riders.

"We go down to the shore here," she called. "Keep in single file and space yourselves out. Charlotte, keep Pie back, clear of Bracken's heels."

"Down to the sand," gasped Sally, suddenly realizing that of course she had always seen the riders on the beach.

"Yes," said Martine. "The horses love it. Gives them a good canter."

"But I don't want to ride on the sand," said Sally.

She felt the terror of her runaway ride on Tarquin tightening her throat and chest. She was sure that this time she would fall off, beneath the galloping hooves of the horses.

"Oh, please," she said. "I don't want to gallop." But Martine was shouting to one of the ladies to stop gossiping and pay attention to her horse.

"Down here," said Martine, leading the way down a steep track that led through the sand dunes and onto the beach.

"No!" screamed Sally inside her head. "I'm not! I'm not!"

But Bilbo was following the black horse with tight, springy strides. He had every intention of having a gallop.

All around Sally was a glistening brightness, the same glare of sea and sand as when Tarquin had run away with her. Suddenly Sally wasn't sure who she was riding. To her taut nerves the solid Bilbo might have been Tarquin.

The whole ride had reached the sand by now. To Sally it seemed as though she were surrounded by plunging horses.

"Steady," warned Martine. "Walk until I tell you to canter. Keep them under control."

"I'm not galloping," shrieked Sally. "Honestly, I'm not!" Her voice vanished into a high squeak.

"Don't be silly," exclaimed Martine, her attention on the other riders. "Bilbo won't go fast."

"I'll wait here," said Sally desperately, and tried to turn the bay horse back to the track.

At the same moment Martine touched her black horse into a slow, controlled canter, keeping the rest of the riders behind her.

Sally tightened her reins, pulling wildly at Bilbo's mouth. The horse fought to follow the others, and Sally knew she couldn't hold him. The only thing she could do was to get off. In a blind panic, she kicked one foot free of her stirrup just as Bilbo tucked down his head and bucked, then went charging after the riders.

At once Martine was calling the riders to stop as she swung her black horse around and came cantering back to Sally. Bilbo ducked and swerved past her, with Sally clinging to the saddle, her mind a blank blur of fear.

Bilbo reached the other riders, who were straggled out across the sand—some slowed to a walk, the two boys still cantering. Sally felt herself slipping, caught a vivid glimpse of Bilbo's shoulder, then the wet sand slapped her with a stinging blow on the side of her face. For seconds Sally lay there, the sand against her eye. Then she scrambled to her feet, telling everyone that she was all right.

Once they made sure that Sally really

wasn't hurt, and after Bilbo came trotting back to investigate, Martine took a leading rein out of her pocket.

"I had no idea you were trying to stop him," she said—annoyed with Sally, annoyed with herself. "Up you go. I'll put a rein on him until we reach the road."

"No. I'm not getting on again. I'm not. I'm not."

"Lead him back to the road then."

"No. I'm not riding again."

Sally was almost surprised at what she was saying. She listened to her voice repeat over and over again that she was not riding.

It took some time to sort out what they were going to do, but in the end the girl on the piebald waited with Sally while the riders—Martine leading Bilbo—went back to the stables to tell Mr. Lorimer that his daughter was waiting to be picked up.

"You should have got on again," said the girl on the piebald scornfully. "You should always get on again after a fall."

Now that it was all over, Sally knew that she had made a total fool of herself. Bilbo wouldn't have run away with her. She had often cantered on Clover at the riding school. It was the memory of Tarquin's galloping that had filled her with such fear.

"I'm going to school for a bit," said the girl on the piebald. "Let me know when your father arrives." She rode away to firmer sand.

Sally went up to wait in the sand dunes by the side of the road, feeling completely miserable.

As she watched for her family's car, a ramshackle, falling-to-bits horse trailer rattled slowly past. A dapple-gray horse looked out from between the slats. In the second that it was driven past, it looked straight at her, and Sally knew she had found her horse.

As Sally gazed after the horse trailer, the Lorimers' car drew up beside her.

"Do you know that horse trailer?" Sally demanded, grabbing open the back door of the car and almost pulling Thalia out. "There, that one."

"It's James Turnball's," said Thalia. "I hate him. He collects old horses, takes them to sales in England, and then you know what happens to them." She spat into the gutter, making Miss Wevell click her tongue disapprovingly and Mr. Lorimer raise his eyebrows in surprise.

Chapter Eight

*I*t seemed a long drive back to Kestrel Manor. Once her father had made sure that Sally hadn't hurt herself, he started talking to Miss Wevell about the books needed for a new branch library. Sally stared out of the window, her arms folded, her shoulders hunched. Thalia tried unsuccessfully to discover exactly what had happened but soon gave up trying.

"But couldn't you have ridden on the road again?" asked her mother when she heard the story.

"I didn't want to," said Sally. "I just didn't want to ride again."

Now that she was safely home, the commonsense part of Sally hardly knew why she hadn't taken Bilbo up to the road and ridden back with the riders. But the hidden, dark part of Sally knew that she would never gallop again. She still wanted a horse as badly as ever. She wanted the gray horse so much that she was sure she would find some way of rescuing it and bringing it to Kestrel Manor. But she was never, ever going to gallop again.

It did not seem a good time to mention the gray horse to her family, so Sally decided that she would find it herself. When she had eaten enough salad and quiche to satisfy her mother, she went down to the stables, hoping to find Thalia there. Jamie and the dogs went too.

"I'm only going to the stable to find Thalia," Sally told Jamie, not wanting to be bothered with him. "You'll get bored."

"I'll find mice," said Jamie. "For Mom."

"You will not. You know she hates them."

"She'll scream," said Jamie happily.

Thalia was cleaning tack. Tarquin was in the field.

"Thought you might have had a nervous breakdown," said Thalia.

"Well, I didn't," said Sally. "All this fuss because I didn't want to gallop."

"Bilbo didn't look to me as if he could gallop," said Thalia, polishing her saddle. "If you hadn't been so silly, you could have had Bilbo here now. We could have been riding together. I think you've changed your mind. You don't want a horse."

"I do, and I know which horse I want. You'll see."

"Well, you'd better be quick. It's the summer holidays in three weeks and then in two weeks it's the gymkhana. You'd better have your horse for that!"

Sally ignored the thought of the gymkhana. She wasn't interested in it. It was bound to mean galloping.

"You know Mr. Turnball—the one whose horse trailer we saw? Where does he live?"

Thalia looked up in surprise at the urgency in Sally's voice.

"Why do you want to know?" she demanded.

"There was a gray horse . . ." Sally began.

"Well, don't go hanging around there," warned Thalia. "It just breaks your heart, that's all it does. He buys old horses and his friend drives them down south to horse auctions. Then they're meat. And you can't stop them because it's legal. And I hate him and I hate everyone who sells their horses to him. So I'm telling you, keep away."

"Where does he live?" Sally repeated. She had been hoping that Thalia would help her save the gray horse, but obviously Thalia wasn't going to become involved with Mr. Turnball.

"You know the farm with the pink walls? You can see it across the fields from the school bus. If you go back toward Fintry Bay, there's a stile with a sign and a public path."

"Oh, yes," said Sally, remembering the sign. "It says 'Craigbet'?"

"That's right. But don't go near him. He's foul. The whole place is utterly foul." Thalia spat on the stone floor.

"You shouldn't spit. It's gross," said Jamie smugly. "I've found one." He held out his plump hand showing them the soft body of a dead vole.

"That's much worse than spitting," said Sally. "Go and bury it."

But seeing that his sister wasn't really too worried about his find, Jamie tucked it into his pocket.

Suddenly Meg and Misty exploded into barking that changed to leaping and wagging as Sally's parents came into the yard.

"So this is where you are," said Sally's mother.

"Look," said Jamie, pulling the vole out of his pocket.

"Throw it away. Now. At once," commanded Mrs. Lorimer.

"I've been telling Sally that she won't have a horse for the gymkhana if she doesn't get a move on," said Thalia.

"I will," said Sally. "You'll see I will. *If* I want to go to the gymkhana, I'll have a horse to ride."

Sally tossed and turned all night. She could think of nothing except the gray horse. At half past five she got up. Looking out of her window, she saw the sea was a polished metal lake and the sky a high dome of dull silver. She took the unicorn from its place on the window ledge and slipped it into her jeans pocket. She would need it to help her find the gray horse.

She took cookies from the jar for herself, two slices of bread and a sliced carrot for the horse, and clipped on Misty's leash, knowing she would bark if she was left behind. She collected Tarquin's halter from its nail by his stall. Tarquin, asleep in the straw, didn't even open an eye. Sally jumped her way down the path to the shore and ran along the sand, watching the other side of the road for the sign to Craigbet.

It was farther than Sally had remembered, but at last she saw it. She climbed over the sand dunes, across the road, over the stile, and then followed the path through the fields at a jog.

By the time she saw the pink-washed farm-house in the distance, her watch said twenty-five to seven. Soon her family would be waking up and wondering where she was.

"They'll think I've taken you for a walk," she said to Misty, who was dragging behind, fed up with being on her leash. But Sally knew that in another half hour they would really start looking for her. She shouldn't be taking Misty for a walk, she should be getting ready for school. She couldn't imagine how getting here had taken her so long.

She ran on until she was close to the farm, then stopped. There didn't seem much point in knocking on Mr. Turnball's door. Sally did not think he would be pleased to see her.

"Now keep close to me," she told Misty, tugging at her leash. "And keep quiet. Don't you dare bark."

Sally crept along the side of a hawthorn hedge, her running shoes filling with muddy water. Halfway down the hedge she saw cattle grazing, but there were no horses with them. As Sally passed them, the cows stopped grazing and followed her along their side of the fence. At the end of the hedge they waited in the corner of the field, watching through long-lashed eyes as Sally climbed over a gate.

Misty made a halfhearted attempt to squeeze through the bars. When Sally tried to pull her through, she lay on her back, paws flopping, eyes rolling.

"It's a good thing you're not Meg," said Sally as she hoisted her over the gate. "I could never have lifted Meg over. Now, come on."

A stream meandered along one side of the field, turning to the right and hidden from Sally's sight by clustering willow trees. But even from the top of the gate Sally had not seen any sign of horses.

"When I saw the gray horse, Mr. Turnball might have been taking it away," she thought suddenly. "Not bringing it here at all. But it must be here. It must."

Sally knew that if the gray horse had been driven south, she would never see it again.

"Don't think about it," she told herself. "Your horse is here." She started to run along the side of the stream. Glancing at her watch, she saw it was almost ten to seven. They would all be really worried about her by now, but she didn't care. She was not going home until she had found her horse.

She ran around the turn of the stream. There, in front of her, were six horses. Sally stopped stock-still. There were three browns, two bays, and a chestnut, all old and weary. But no gray horse. Tears of disappointment filled Sally's eyes. Where would she look now? Then she saw a movement in the clump of willows at the side of the stream.

Under the green shadows of the weeping willows the gray horse was standing alone, watching Sally.

"Oh, horse!" cried Sally. She could only stand and wait as the horse walked slowly toward her, its wide nostrils trembling with a silent whinnying welcome.

The horse was small, about fourteen hands

high. A dapple-gray mare, her ribs showed through her harsh coat. Her neck was sunken, and her quarters were flat. Her long white mane and tail drifted as she walked. She had an Araby dished face and huge Arab eyes. As she walked toward Sally, she dragged her near hind leg, and Sally saw it was torn from the point of her quarters to below her hock.

Sally pushed her hand under the horse's long mane, stroked her neck, and ran her hand over the bony shoulders, telling the horse that she loved her.

"Dad will buy you for me," Sally whispered. "We'll come for you tonight."

Cautiously she took the carrot slices out of her pocket, offering them secretly to the horse so that the other horses wouldn't see.

Very gently the gray horse took a slice of carrot from Sally's hand. Sheer happiness filled Sally's whole being.

"You'll love Kestrel Manor," she told the gray horse. Then, suddenly, Misty plunged forward, splitting the silence with her barking.

Sally looked up from the horse to see a small, dark-haired man walking toward her. He was wearing heavy rubber boots, soiled jeans, and a filthy tweed jacket. His face was dark with unshaven beard and his beady eyes were fixed on Sally.

"And what do you think you're up to?" he demanded, walking closer to Sally.

Misty lifted her lips, revealing pink gums and crocodile teeth. She snarled from the depths of her throat. The man stood still.

"I came to see the gray horse," said Sally.

"Thought my farm was a public park, eh?"

"I want to buy her," said Sally, her voice sounding shaky.

"Do you now? Well, I dare say that could be arranged. I'm in the business of selling horse-flesh. You'll need to be quick, though. I've come to bring them in. Two hours from now and this little lot will be off on their summer holiday."

Sally kept her arm over the gray horse's withers. Her other hand clutched tightly onto Misty's lead. As long as she had Misty, she felt sure the man, who she supposed was Mr. Turnball, wouldn't come any closer.

"Please keep the gray horse," she pleaded. "Don't send her away with the others. Dad will pay for her tonight. Honest he will. You must keep her for me."

"I'd have my fields full of little horses waiting for the likes of you to bring me their money. You want her, you have the cash in my hand before ten this morning or she'll be gone with the rest. Now get off with you."

Sally swung blindly away. Dragging Misty behind her, she ran across the pebbly stream and went full tilt across the fields in the direction of Kestrel Manor. Not keeping to the paths or stiles, she raced furiously on.

It was almost twenty-five past seven by her watch. Her father and Ben left the house at around a quarter to eight. Her only hope of saving the gray horse was to catch her father and persuade him to come to Mr. Turnball's now. It was no use asking her mother. She would only say, Wait until your father comes home—and by then it would be too late.

Misty stopped at a sudden smell, pulling her head out of her collar, but Sally hardly paused. Every second was vital. She stuffed Misty's collar and leash into her pocket, felt her forgotten unicorn, and, grasping it in her hand, ran desperately on, hoping to reach the road to Kestrel Manor's gates before her father did.

At last she saw the gray strip of road, the beach grass, and the washed line of the sea. Her breath burned in her lungs and her legs staggered as she forced herself to keep going.

It was almost a quarter to eight when the gates of Kestrel Manor came into sight. Only a field of rough grass, spiked with gorse bushes, lay between her and home. Staring at the open, rusted gates, Sally ran mechanically on, knowing that it was possible her father and Ben had gone. That she was already too late.

Their car came down the avenue as Sally was halfway across the field.

"Stop!" she screamed. "Stop. Dad, stop!"

Sally raced wildly to the road, yelling her loudest and waving her arms above her head. Her foot caught on the root of a gorse bush and she fell flat on the ground.

At the gates of Kestrel Manor, Mr. Lorimer paused to check the road and, turning right, drove off to Tarent.

By the time Sally had scrambled to her feet, the car was out of sight.

Chapter Nine

Sally ran on blindly, as if there were still hope, as if she had seen the car only in her imagination. She climbed over the stone wall, crossed the road, and stood in Kestrel Manor's gateway, tears running down her face, not knowing what she was going to do now.

A car swung into the drive, swerved to avoid Sally, then skidded to a halt.

"Sally!" roared her father as he burst out of the car. "What on earth are you doing here?"

Sally stared unbelievingly, then flung herself into her father's arms, sobbing out her story.

"Please, she is the horse I want. She is the horse I would like. Please come back now, at once, or she'll be gone. He said we have to be there before ten."

"Calm down," said Mr. Lorimer, offering Sally his handkerchief. "Here, mop yourself up. I'd be well on my way to work by now if it hadn't been for Misty."

Blowing her nose, Sally looked at the car
and realized that Misty was sitting in the backseat. Ben was gripping her ruff, his attention on
his book.

"She got away from me."

"We found her sniffing along the road.
Caught her and turned to bring her back. So it's
Misty you've got to thank. Now, get in and let's
see what we can do. You are sure this is the
horse you want?"

"Really sure," said Sally when she was
established in the backseat beside Misty. "More
than wanting the dentist to stop drilling."

"If you really are certain," said her father.
Ben said it didn't matter if he was a bit late, it
was only gym.

Mr. Lorimer drove to Craigbet farm. He told
Sally to stay where she was and crossed the lit-
tered yard to knock on the farm door.

Sally could hardly believe what was hap-
pening. It had all changed so suddenly from
total despair to the hope that in a few minutes
the gray horse would be hers.

Mr. Turnball came to the door and spoke
with her father. Then they walked across the

yard together and Mr. Turnball pushed open a barn door. He went in, and came out leading the gray horse by a coarse rope around her neck.

"Is this the one?" asked Mr. Lorimer.

"Yes," said Sally, getting out of the car. The gray horse turned her delicate, wildflower face and riffled her nostrils, knowing Sally.

"Right," said her father. "You have chosen." He took out his checkbook.

Mr. Turnball tossed the rope in Sally's direction as he scuttled to Mr. Lorimer's side to discuss the price. Sally fitted Tarquin's halter around the gray horse's head and knotted it securely, telling the horse she was safe now.

"Pleasure to do business with you," said Mr. Turnball to her father. Mr. Lorimer smiled politely and told Sally that if she could lead the horse he would drive slowly in front of her.

The car bumped over the potholes in the farm road. Sally walked beside her horse, for this short time completely happy, wanting nothing else in the whole world.

Mr. Lorimer went slowly along the road, turned down the avenue, and drove to Kestrel Manor. Hearing the car, Mrs. Lorimer, Jamie, and Meg came rushing out. The gray horse stood at Sally's side, looking about her with mild interest. She didn't even flinch when the Beardies bounded around her.

"Where have you been?" demanded her mother. "I've been so worried about you."

Sally and Mr. Lorimer explained.

"You should have left a note," said Mrs. Lorimer. "No, I'm not listening to any excuses. And what about school?"

"Yes," said Ben from the car. "I don't mind missing gym, but I've got to be there for social studies."

"Right, we're off," said Mr. Lorimer, and they drove away.

"The poor pony's got a sore leg," said Jamie. "It's all bleeding."

Guiltily Sally remembered her horse's leg.

"She wasn't lame when I was leading her," she said hurriedly.

"Looks nasty to me," said her mother. "I'll phone the vet."

"And school? I don't need to go today, do I?"

Mrs. Lorimer hugged her daughter to her. "Well," she said. "Just this once."

"Does she look very old?" said Sally anxiously.

"Well . . . thin," said her mother. "Tired, too. Whatever made you pick her?"

"Love," said Sally.

Dr. Cheever, the vet, was young, with longish hair, purple jeans, and a gaudy T-shirt. He said the cut wasn't deep and fortunately not infected. He gave the gray horse two injections, which made Sally curl her toes but didn't seem to bother the horse at all.

"Is she very old?" asked Sally, deciding it was better to know than to go on worrying about it.

"Old?" said the vet. "Oh, six, seven."

A grin of relief spread across Sally's face.

"She's in poor condition, but nothing that a few weeks of good feeding won't fix. You've got a very nice horse. You'll be riding her in a week or two. Will I be seeing you at the gymkhana? I'm the official vet."

Sally wanted to say no, she didn't think she would be at the gymkhana, but the vet had turned to Mrs. Lorimer and was talking to her about feed and the best place to buy it.

"Right," he said, packing up his bag and pushing Misty away. "I'll drop by tomorrow, give her another injection. Keep her in until I see her again."

"Thank you for coming," said Sally as the vet and her mother went back to Kestrel Manor.

Sally laid her arms along the top of the half door, resting her chin on her hands. In her mind's eye she saw the horse watching her from under the willow trees.

"Willow," said Sally. "That's your name. Willow." The gray horse turned to look inquiringly at Sally, almost as if she knew her name.

Thalia came straight from school.

"What a beautiful horse!" she exclaimed. "Super! When she's fit, she'll be as fast as Tarquin! We can have the best summer ever. We can jump and gallop and ride over to the Tarent show, and we can go in for the pairs jumping at the cross-country. . . ."

Thalia's face was alight with enthusiasm, but Sally turned quickly away. She felt fear twist in the pit of her stomach and tighten her head. For a split second she was riding Tarquin again, being carried away in a helpless blur of terror.

"The vet doesn't know when she'll be fit to ride."

"Four weeks to the gymkhana," said Thalia. "She'll be fit for the games."

The vet came again the next day. He gave Willow another injection and said she could go out during the day, that the grass would be the best thing for her.

On Thursday evening he dropped in to check up on her. Sally had tied Willow to the gatepost of the field and was brushing out her mane with a dandy brush while Thalia rode Tarquin in schooling circles at a sitting trot. Mr. Lorimer, Jamie, and the vet walked down to the field.

"Let's see the patient," said the vet, examining Willow's cut, which had scabbed over. "Good. No heat at all, and she's looking much better. No reason why you shouldn't start riding her. Take it easy to begin with."

"Will Sally be able to ride her at the gymkhana?" Thalia asked the vet.

"Oh, yes. No problem," said the vet, waving good-bye.

"There you are," triumphed Thalia. "You can come."

"Need to wait and see," said Sally, avoiding Thalia's eyes.

They measured Willow for a saddle and bridle, and on Sunday, Miss Wevell drove up to Kestrel Manor with the trunk of her car stacked with tack borrowed from a friendly saddler.

Willow stood patiently in her stall while Miss Wevell fitted saddles and bridles. "There," she announced at last. "That's a nice broad snaffle and that saddle looks good to me. Up you go and we'll see what it's like with you on top."

"It's the first time Sally's ridden her," said Ben, who was watching with the rest of the family and Thalia.

"Take it easy, then," said Miss Wevell, and held Willow's bridle while Sally mounted. But the horse made no fuss. Miss Wevell squinted under the saddle to make sure it wasn't resting on Willow's spine, then told Sally to ride her around the yard. Sally gathered up the reins, squeezed her legs against Willow's sides, and there she was, riding her own horse.

Fizzy with happiness, Sally rode down to the field and walked Willow around. The horse seemed as happy as Sally as she walked out with a long, balanced stride. Sally asked her for a trot and she trotted out confidently, settling back to a walk the minute Sally asked her to.

"Go on," shouted Thalia. "Canter."

Sally walked Willow over to the gate.

"No," she said quickly. "She's not fit to canter." Miss Wevell told her to stand still while she checked the saddle again.

Sally got up very early the next morning and rode Willow in the field by herself. Willow walked quietly around, enjoying the early-morning stillness with ears pricked and eyes bright.

"We'll just ride by ourselves to begin with," Sally told Willow, patting her shoulder and leaning forward to press her cheek against the horse's neck.

Even when vacation started, Sally still rode

by herself in the early mornings. During the day she helped Thalia set up jumps for Tarquin or watched her schooling. Thalia, long-legged and totally sure that there was nothing Tarquin couldn't do, made it all look so easy.

"She would gallop and jump anything," Sally thought, watching enviously.

A week before the gymkhana Thalia appeared at Kestrel Manor with the entry forms.

"These have to be filled in and mailed today," she announced, plonking herself down on the stairs.

"I'm not going," said Sally. "I've told you."

"Well, I'm entering you for the games," said Thalia, filling in the form. "Willow is perfectly fit. You're bound to change your mind."

But although Willow was beginning to look sleek and rounded, Sally did not change her mind. Even on the night before the gymkhana, when she was sitting on her bedroom window seat looking out over the long stretch of sand to the white tents of the gymkhana field, Sally knew that going to the gymkhana would mean galloping. And she was never, ever going to gallop again.

"You'd love to go," accused the voice in her head.

"I would not," Sally replied instantly. "I am never, ever going to gallop again. Not ever." And she held the crystal unicorn up to the dim evening light, a brightness in her hand.

Chapter Ten

S ally stood on the steps of Kestrel Manor, her hands behind her back, her nails digging into her palms to keep herself from crying.

"I'm sure. I'm quite sure. I don't want to come with you," she said.

All her family except Ben, who was in Tarent, were sitting in the car. Meg was in the back, panting. They were on their way to join Thalia at the gymkhana.

Sally had spent her morning trying to help Thalia get Tarquin ready for the gymkhana. Thalia had kept saying that it was quite all right, she could manage, and if Sally wanted to groom a horse why didn't she groom Willow?

"We would all so much rather you came with us," said her mother. "But if you really don't want to come, you can go on searching for Misty. Now, don't do anything silly. We'll be back about five. Oh, Sally, come on. Jump in."

"No," Sally said, and turned away quickly,

going back into the house so that they wouldn't see her eyes filling with tears.

"I don't care," she thought. "The last thing I want to do is to ride at their rotten gymkhana. I'd rather ride here by myself. Much rather."

But all the time she was wishing that she had gone with Thalia, riding together to the gymkhana, with Tarquin and Willow all spruced up.

"But you're safe here," Sally told herself. "You won't have to gallop here."

For a while Sally searched the grounds for Misty, shouting about the dinners, walks, and chocolate cookies that were waiting for her if she would only come home. But there was no trace of Misty. No hairy face covered with grasses and leaves peered through the undergrowth. No pad of paws announced her return. Ben had taken the dogs out that morning and Misty had done her usual disappearing trick. They had been in the walled garden. One second Misty had been with him, the next she was gone.

At last Sally gave up. She brought Willow in, meaning to ride down the avenue and search for Misty there. She groomed Willow, put on her tack, then went to get her hard hat from her room. She climbed the stairs, smoothing the carved kestrels as she passed. She took her hard hat from its hook behind the door, then sat down on the window seat. Sea and sand stretched to blue sky, and Sally was alone in the whole of Kestrel Manor. Brightly colored flags fluttered from the gymkhana tents. They would all be there now.

Instantly Sally looked away from the gymkhana. She searched the grounds of Kestrel Manor and the fields beyond for any disturbance that might be Misty. But there was no sign of her.

"Thalia thinks you're a coward," Sally told herself. "Afraid of everything. But it's not true. It's not true."

Sally picked up the crystal unicorn and set it in the center of her hand, just as it had been when she had found it. She looked at it closely, giving it all her attention. Suddenly she knew what she would do.

She would climb the tower. Her parents had forbidden any of them to go near the tower until the stairs were rebuilt, but Sally didn't care. She jumped down from the window seat and ran downstairs. Taking the stepladder from the kitchen, she clanged her way back up and set the ladder squarely under the trapdoor. She clambered up, then hesitated. What would her mother say if she could see her now? But her mother would never know. No one would know. She had to climb the tower to prove to herself that she wasn't a coward.

Sally pushed the heavy trapdoor open. When the dust settled, she could see the stairs and the patch of blue sky above her head.

She took a deep breath, gritted her teeth, and pulled herself up through the trapdoor to sit at the foot of the tower. The wood of the stairs was worse than Sally had remembered, but the metal banister seemed firm enough. Sally stood up cautiously and gripped the rusty metal. She shook it hard. Tatters of wood fell down, but the banister did not move. Holding on to the rail, Sally slowly made her way upward.

As she climbed she heard wood and plaster falling down beneath her. A lump of rotted wood fell through the trapdoor and crashed to the floor below. For a minute Sally could not move—she could only cling helplessly, her hands sticky with sweat, her mouth and throat bone-dry.

"Go on, Sally Lorimer. Go on."

Trembling, Sally forced herself to move one foot to the next rung, and then the next.

At last she reached the top. It was easy to step from the banister to the broad stone platform that surrounded the tower.

Sally gazed out in total amazement. She felt she could almost see around the curve of the globe—ocean and fields, farms, rough lawns, clumps of trees, and church spires lay spread out beneath her. She could see beyond the gymkhana field to meadows and roads and white country houses.

Looking away from the view, Sally saw that there was a small metal chest on the platform. Cautiously she made her way around to it. To her surprise it opened easily and was quite dry inside. As well as maps, playing cards, and books, there was a pair of binoculars in a leather case. Sally slipped the leather strap over her head. Holding the binoculars to her eyes, she focused the blurred colors until the landscape leaped at her. She could see shells on the shore, blades of grass, and the petals of flowers. She turned the binoculars to the gymkhana and saw horses and riders, red-and-white poles, and a black horse jumping. She saw sandwiches and lemonade on a trestle table, and someone who could only be Thalia's narg ready to sell them.

She followed the line of the shore back toward Kestrel Manor. A rough field reached down to the shore. A fence made of strands of wire surrounded it. Something was caught beneath the bottom strand of the wire, struggling to free itself. Its long gray-and-white hair fanned out as it threw itself desperately against the wire.

Sally focused the glasses on it, and there was Misty, so close that Sally felt she could almost touch her. Her eyes were wild with panic and her front feet clawed frantically at her neck. As Sally stared, hardly able to believe what she was seeing, Misty gave a sudden violent leap, then fell back from the wire and hung there motionless, so still she might have been dead.

Sally screamed Misty's name, dropped the binoculars back into their case, slammed the lid shut, and was groping, stumbling her way down the banister, jumping onto the ladder, and leaping down to the floor at panic speed.

There was no one she could phone, no one to help her. The police were too far away and too slow.

"Misty," Sally cried again. "Oh, Misty."

Somehow Sally had to reach her and take her to a vet. Then she remembered that the vet would be at the gymkhana. There was only one way to reach him. She had to gallop Willow across the beach to Misty and find some way of taking her to the vet.

For a moment Sally was frozen with terror. Her legs would not move. She had to do the thing she dreaded most—to gallop across the beach. But it was for Misty. In her mind's eye she saw the limp, hanging body. For Misty. And Sally drove the stupid fear out of her mind.

She spun into her room, grabbed her hard hat, thrust the unicorn deep into her pocket, and tore downstairs. In the kitchen she snatched the kitchen scissors, dragged on her jacket, and flew down to the stables.

"We've got to reach her now, at once," Sally cried as she pulled up Willow's girth and rushed her into the yard. Sally sprang into the saddle as if she were Thalia and pushed Willow into a canter as they plunged down the sandy track to the shore.

"Go on! Go on!" Sally cried. There was no space for fear, nothing in her head but the desperate need to reach Misty.

Willow's hooves pounded into the sand. Her long mane and tail bannered about her as Sally crouched low and tight over her neck, urging her on.

They reached the field where Misty was trapped, and Sally pulled Willow to a plunging halt. She threw herself from the saddle and looped Willow's reins over one of the fence posts. Then she flung herself across the field to where Misty hung unconscious from the wire fence. Sally crouched down beside her and saw that she had put her head through a nylon noose-shaped trap that hung from the bottom strand of wire. Sally's fingers searched desperately through Misty's thick ruff of hair until she found the nylon noose. She cut through it with the scissors, and Misty's limp body fell to the ground.

Sally stared down helplessly. Misty's eyes were closed and her tongue lolled from the side of her mouth, her breath harsh and uneven. She was still alive.

"The vet," Sally thought. "Got to get her to the vet. Now."

Hardly knowing what she was going to do, Sally pulled off her jacket, spread it out, and laid Misty on top of it. She zipped it up and knotted the sleeves together. Carrying the warm, limp body in her arms, she staggered back to Willow.

"It's only Misty," she told the gray horse. "Only Misty. You know her. It's all right." Willow breathed over the strange bundle, then whinnied gently, letting Sally know that she understood.

Somehow Sally hoisted Misty over her horse's withers, somehow held her there as she scrambled back into the saddle. Clutching

Misty, she managed to turn Willow back to the beach.

"Gallop," Sally told her. "Go on, gallop. You've got to get us to the gymkhana, got to get us to the vet," she urged Willow on.

Sally had thought she could hold on to Misty with one hand and the reins with the other, but it took both hands to stop the lolling, unconscious Beardie from falling off. Sally had to leave the reins loose and was able to guide Willow only with her legs.

Straight and true, Willow galloped across the sand, never hesitating or trying to turn back. She raced up the short lane to the gymkhana field and plunged through the entrance.

"I've got to see the vet," Sally screamed at the amazed spectators. "It's urgent, really urgent!" In seconds Dr. Cheever stood beside her. He lifted Misty up out of the jacket and carried her to his Land Rover. He laid her down on the grass and examined her.

"It was a noose," Sally explained as she slackened Willow's girth, eased her saddle, and patted her neck, praising her and thanking her for her bold galloping. "Some sort of trap."

"I'd like to hang whoever did this from their own noose," swore the vet.

"Is she all right? Is she going to be all right?" Sally demanded.

"Her thick coat's saved her. If she were a smooth-coated dog, you'd have lost her," he answered.

He took a syringe out of his case, filled it, and injected Misty.

"That will give her heart a bit of a boost. She'll come around in a few moments."

"It's Sally," yelled Thalia as she trotted Tarquin toward them. "What's happened?" she asked. "What's wrong with Misty?"

Sally blurted out her story.

"You mean you galloped across the beach?" exclaimed Thalia, ignoring everything else. "You really galloped?"

Thalia went to find Sally's parents, and by the time she returned with them Misty had opened her eyes, sat up, scratched herself, and peed.

"She'll be all right," said the vet. "Keep her quiet for a bit and keep an eye on her from now on. You were lucky this time. Next time you could be too late. I'll call in this evening and check up on her."

Sally repeated her story, and her mother said they would talk about climbing the tower stairs later.

"But Sally galloped," insisted Thalia. "She's not afraid any longer."

Sally listened to their praises, not really hearing them. What mattered was that she had escaped from the blackness of being afraid, that Misty was safe, and that Willow, her own horse, was the best possible horse in the whole world.

They were on their way back to the Lorimers' car, Misty walking beside Meg as if nothing had happened to her, Jamie with a lollipop in each hand, when Thalia shouted, "Musical poles! They've not started yet and I entered Sally."

In minutes Sally found herself trotting around the ring with twelve other children, ready to ride into the center and put her hard hat on a pole when the tape stopped playing. Willow listened to the music, spun around, and cantered to a pole the second it stopped. She kept Sally in until fourth place. Sally's ribbon, her first ribbon, was yellow with gold lettering. Thalia's was blue for second place.

When the gymkhana was over, Sally and Thalia rode home together. Mrs. Lorimer had invited Thalia and Narg for a picnic supper in the summerhouse.

"We'll need to see about our entries for the Tarent Horse Show," said Thalia. "I'll ask my narg to find out about them."

"Oh, yes," agreed Sally, then stopped, giggling at herself. She hadn't even thought of being afraid.

"Do you think Willow can jump?" Thalia asked. "She looks to me as if she could."

"Well, I can't," said Sally.

"Of course you can," said Thalia. "Jumping's easy as long as your horse enjoys it. I'll show you."

As they walked their horses slowly back to Kestrel Manor, Sally's imagination was dazzled with thoughts of jumping Willow, of the Tarent show, and of her crystal unicorn, secure in her pocket, that seemed to have cast its rainbow magic over her whole life.

"Thank you," she said aloud. "Thank you." And she rode through sky- and sea-light home to Kestrel Manor and a future filled with horses.